MW01100571

The Land of Golden Sunshine

An Allegory of Soul-Yearning

J. Donald Walters
Illustrations by Haripriya Dillon

Revised second edition
Copyright © 2002 by Hansa Trust
All rights reserved

Printed in Canada
ISBN: 1-56589-190-2

Cover design by C. A. Starner Schuppe

Crystal Clarity Publishers
14618 Tyler-Foote Road
Nevada City, CA 95959

Phone: 800-424-1055 or 530-478-7600
Fax: 530-478-7610

www.crystalclarity.com
clarity@crystalclarity.com

*Have you ever felt the call
To soar on wings of inner freedom?
If so, it's to you, Friend,
That this book is dedicated.*

Introduction

This little story, more than anything else I've ever written in words—more deeply even than my autobiography, *The Path*—is an expression of who I am, inside. My music does it also—much of it—but no other literary work.

I don't know how many are interested in gaining this insight. I've never liked to intrude myself on others, for I realize that I'm not of any real importance in this world. No one is! I do know, of course, that I've done a few things in my life. A few people have kindly expressed appreciation for some of them. Inside me, however, I've never felt defined by any of them. One has no choice but to be active in this life, and I've tried to be of some help to others. Inside myself, however, those activities haven't touched me. They've never expressed who I really am.

I've traveled far and wide in this world. When meeting strangers, my principal perception of us has been that we are fellow seekers of truths for which we all hunger, behind all the "busyness" of our lives. My own self-definition has always been in terms of this inner aspiration.

The "mood" of this book was mine at five and six years of age. It was mine at the age of eighteen, when I wrote it. Nearly sixty years have passed since then; I'm what people call an "old man" now, though I don't feel it. Nor did I ever feel young. I'm like Lisa, the simple girl in this story. Her "mood" today is still mine.

We are all strangers in this world. We may try to make it our own, but it can never be ours. Alone we came into it.

And alone we must leave it. And all we can take with us when we leave is the longing in our hearts to embrace LIFE with deeper understanding.

In divine friendship,
J. Donald Walters

⟐ One ⟐

The November wind-hordes camped
Outside the tensely waiting city.
For a few days their scouts—
Dark, lowering giants from the north—
Roamed the skies restlessly overhead,
Searching out every weakness
In the city's defenses.

Shrill-laughing eddies of wind
Reveled riotously through the forest,
Toasting their coming victory
With back-slapping gusts,
While drunken flurries of dust
Caroused through the coarse meadow grasses,
Chanting wildly of warfare
And cruel conquest.

At last, worked up
Into a destructive fury,
The invaders swept
Shouting through the city,
Swinging sharp, icy blades that bit deep
Into the flesh of the inhabitants.

These helpless unfortunates
Huddled in little groups
On street corners, and,
Through chattering teeth,
Passed fearful comments
On the days ahead—
Words which the wind-hordes took up
And tossed mockingly from group to
     group.

Then, suddenly, the invaders were gone.
The city dwellers glanced up in relief
At a cloudless sky, and prayed
That they might enjoy yet a few more days
Of the fast-dwindling warmth.

A week passed.
Then a fresh host appeared from the north—
Wilder, more savage than the first.
Drunk with the lust for conquest
(Though the city cowered already
In abject submission)
The new wave of barbarians swept howling
Through the unresisting streets,
Cutting—
Pillaging—
Destroying everywhere.

Then, quite as suddenly—
They too were gone.

And so the month of November passed.
And the city's inhabitants knew
That every fresh wave from the north
Brought them ever closer to the triumphal
        entry of
The Snow-Earl,
And they were afraid.

⁜═⁜ Two ⁜═⁜

In the city
There was a brown-walled factory,
With high, dusty windows
On a windy street,
Where a hundred women worked
At making men's shirts.
Most had worked there for many years,
And would continue there
Until their eyes grew old,
Their faces lined and tired,
Grim-mouthed with disillusionment.

Sometimes (not often)
A young woman left to get married.
Ah, then—what buzzing excitement
        there was!
(And what a poignant contrast it made
To the normal apathy.)
A few of the women were even glad—
For a few days—
In their co-worker's good fortune.
But many others, alas! envied her
In their shriveled hearts.

And the bride?
Oh, she left, happy and proud.
And settled down comfortably—
Alas! however, to yet another life of drudgery,
As her dreams lay scattered about her feet
Like dry leaves.

For after a time—
As smoke, rising from the chimneys,
Is dispersed by November's winds—
Her happiness drifted away,
And the years once again
Swirled past her, unnoticed,
Like eddies of dust.

No one in the city was happy.
Oh, there was brittle laughter—
And what passes among desperate people
For merriment.
But happiness?
Go there: See for yourself.

Yet it was in this factory
That Lisa worked:
Lisa—thrice visited, thrice called
By the golden sun-man.

One person alone knows the story directly:
An older worker in the factory,
And Lisa's only close acquaintance.
(Alas! no one in that loveless city,
Has any real friends!)
But this woman, old by this time,
Seldom repeats the tale.

Lisa worked in the center of the large floor,
At a solid wooden table
With nine other women.
Together, from morning till closing time,
Their duty was to sew buttons
Of many shapes, colors, and sizes
Onto men's shirts.

Lisa was young—
Simple-hearted, and kind,
With eyes that still knew how to smile.

Two years earlier she had begun working
        there,
To support her aged mother.
Then one day, some months ago,
The old woman had died.
(Had her soul gone anywhere?—
Who knew? Who, except Lisa, even cared?)
But the young girl—
Lacking another focus for her life—
Worked on, not really aware of the drudgery—
Existing from week to week,
Like all the others,
For the refuge of each coming Sunday.

Sunday was their day of rest.
Late that morning with heavy eyelids,
They might shake off slumber,
Drink something warm,
And glance idly at photographs
In some cheap magazine.
Then, usually, they slept again.

This, forever, was the best
They asked of life—
Escape, each Sunday, from reality—
Escape into the hazy peace
That people find who have forgotten
How to walk on clouds of gold.

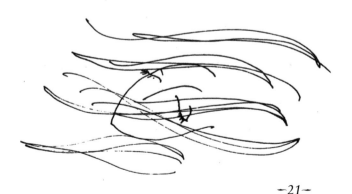

The second week in November ended.
Several days had passed
In a gaunt procession
Of icy wind and rain.

As the factory's closing time drew near,
The large room where Lisa worked
Stirred with restless chatter,
And thoughts of the freezing journey home
Were mitigated by welcome thoughts
Of their day of rest ahead—
Sunday, their day of nothingness:
Their day of sleep!

The hands on the faded clock moved
Steadily, with the impartiality of destiny.
Until at last the bell sounded:
Five o'clock!
A hundred women,
Stirred to motion like ripples on a pond,
Rose from their tables.
Jostling forward in an impatient line,
They punched the time clock,
Gathered shawls, gloves, and coats,
And hurried home.

Lisa, since her mother's death,
Had rented quarters
In an older part of the city—
An inexpensive attic room,
Poorly heated,
With one sloping window—almost a
    skylight—
In a grey, slated roof.

Sometimes on Sunday morning,
When heavy skies, for a brief hour or two,
Parted their veils, and allowed the sun
To smile upon the city
With brief, much-needed warmth,
A shaft of sunlight, pale but friendly,
Would slant down into Lisa's room,
For a time bringing light
To Lisa's heart.

The room's furnishings were few and old—
Though good enough, I dare say,
For the comfort of a poor girl:
A small, worn rug that clung fearfully
To the center of the floor,
A wobbly table,
Two chairs,
And a spring bed which creaked
  complainingly
Whenever Lisa, stretched upon it,
Turned to the wall to escape her thoughts
Of the city.

Reaching her room, she shut the door,
And glanced around her
As if with the silent question,
"Is this all?"
The cold room, the chair—
The emptiness—
Answered her even more silently.
She then gazed up through the high, slop-
      ing window.
For a moment, her thoughts soared
Into the vast evening sky.

Preparing a light supper, then,
She ate a small sandwich
And sat at the table,
Listening to the silent, gathering night.
An hour passed. Then,
Moved suddenly by a strange expectancy,
She got into bed and gazed up again
Through the slanting window.

Night, that compassionate thief,
Crept stealthily over the housetops,
Snaring men's cares and fears
In his soft net of slumber.

The rain and wind,
Tired of their attack on the defenseless city,
Moved on in search of new prey
In distant lands.

A few bright stars peered timidly
Through the ragged, flapping trains
Of vanishing clouds;
Then, bolder, they came out,
And beckoned to their smaller sisters.
Soon they all joined together, laughing,
In a game of hide-and-seek,
While stern, lingering vapors,
Dignity affronted,
Gathered their garments about them
And hastened grimly
Toward the horizon.

After a time rose the moon.
And earth and heaven,
Long battered by the raging storm,
Drank deep of the cool,
Still,
Revivifying light.

Through the sloping window of Lisa's room
A wide ray of moonlight
Descended to the floor,
Drenching it in peace.
Awaking, she saw it,
And smiled.

Somewhere in the distance a bird sang,
Seeming, to the young girl,
To be telling tales of undying love—
Of shining happiness.

Ah! she thought, if only life
Would really offer such blessings!
Was pure love even possible?
Was happiness?

Did anyone exist—
Anywhere on earth—
To whom these ideals
Were more than dreams?

A pang of yearning stabbed her heart,
Its sharp pain bringing tears to her eyes.
How long she had known this yearning!
Like a flute at twilight,
Playing its lonely notes on a distant hill,
This yearning had haunted her, and
Had been with her always:
Deeply it underlay the long, rolling years,
The days—the endless-seeming months
Of her young life.

Tonight, however, some subtle change
Seemed to be wafting on the night breeze
With that lonely melody,
As though the flute notes were dancing.
Was some kindly shepherd playing
To listening ears somewhere—
To listening thoughts—
To listening, answering smiles?
A hint it seemed, no more—
But the melody of yearning through the years
Was laden suddenly
With a new, a very special message!

What was its purport?
Was it of hope?
Was that slight rising
At the end of each line
A hint of some smiling promise?

Tonight, the young girl saw herself all at once
A creature of the city no longer.
To herself she seemed a butterfly
Struggling for release
From its cocoon!

Free and soaring, she felt as if
She were joining in laughter with the comets,
Leaping lightly over distant star-clouds;
Drinking thirstily with light rays
Of the moon,
And sipping at fountains of eternal joy!

Sleep caught her again,
Rocking her gently
In its cloud-arms of peace.

Meanwhile, the pale ray of moonlight
Moved slowly onward,
Flowed over the old, uneven boards—
Caressed with magic fingers
The shabby walls, the old and worn
        furniture,
And touched the bed lightly
Whereon Lisa lay.

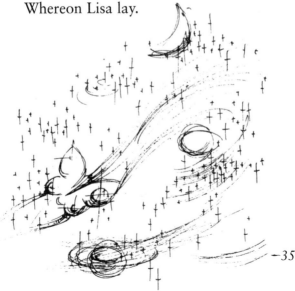

❧ Three ❧

    Lisa awoke with a start
And sat up.
A glance at a clock by her bed told her
That it was already late.
Soon, the sun would reach its zenith;
Light filled the window,
Though slightly dimmed by a passing cloud.

    Everything seemed watchful in anticipation.
A quiet sense of excitement gripped the still air
As though eager to tell it something.

Lisa hardly dared to breathe.
Turning, she sat motionless
On the edge of the bed.

A dove flew by outside,
Its wing-beats quickly fading away.
In that mystical hush
The rustling passage
Seemed almost an omen.

Then the cloud was gone,
And the room brightened:
A wide ray of sunlight—
Warm and quiet—
Poured through the sloping window
Like a shower of gold
Onto the floor.

What was it, this day,
That impressed Lisa so strangely?
The beams of sunlight shone
With some subtle power!

Minutes passed. Then,
In the steady flow of light,
Fresh waves of radiance—
As of some alien substance—
Shimmered downward,
Landing in the pool of gold on the floor.

The light of the room
Was drawn as if magnetically
Into this shining column.

In the center of that luminescence
An apparition slowly began
To take shape.

At last—
A cloudlike human form appeared:
It was vaguely moving.
A misty arm seemed
Stretched out in blessing,
Fingers merging into diaphanous light.
A bright sun-burst about the head
Condensed into shining,
Golden hair.

   Where luminous cascades
Had seemed to swirl gracefully to the floor,
A flowing white robe now appeared,
Spirally draped.

And there at last stood
The most beautiful being Lisa had ever seen.
A man?
But surely it was an angel!
Strength, suggested in that firm bearing,
Was softened in the eyes
By an expression of compassionate love.
Wisdom in the high forehead
Was sweetened by a smile
That hinted at whole realms
Of inner joy.

Lisa knelt instinctively in adoration.
Words seemed superfluous.
But, oh, her heart sang!

Divine peace, like a refreshing,
Weightless waterfall,
Overwhelmed her.

Love, almost the bearer of pain,
Filled her heart.

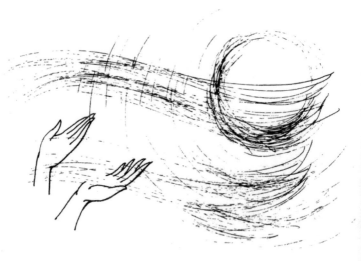

How long she remained there
She could not have told.

But the sun,
Making its slow arc through the sky,
Moved the pool of light on the floor
Nearer and nearer—
To the spot where Lisa,
With bursting heart, knelt.

Suddenly,
As she gazed at his feet,
She found herself encircled
In the golden aureole of lambent light
That surrounded him!
Startled, almost afraid,
She glanced up.

And the sun's rays struck her
Full in the face.

Alas! that too-penetrating brilliance!
Tightly she closed her eyelids,
And quickly lowered her head.

When she looked up again—
He was gone!
Wildly she looked around:
He had vanished.

The sunlight had lost
Its magic quality;
Her room, poor and plain
As it had been before,
Whispered no echo of the melody that,
Only moments before,
Had touched it so wondrously.

At first, Lisa felt stranded—
As though lost in a tunnel of night.
Had the sun-man appeared so briefly—
Only to abandon her forever?

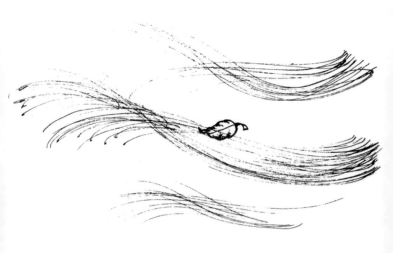

But then the memory of her experience,
Like a mighty wave,
Burst on her anew.

"Love *exists!*" she thought,
Wonder-struck at the revelation.
"Joy *exists!*"

New doors of transcendent meaning
Seemed to be opening
Onto the vast universe around her.
It was as though life itself, for her,
Had dawned only
With the sun's light, today.

And though, outwardly,
The world gave no sign that it was changed,
Never more for her, she felt,
Would it be the same.

Her bare room, humble as it still was,
Seemed drab no longer,
But sweet in its simplicity,
And gently unassuming.
Her work at the factory,
Humdrum as she had good reason to think it,
Seemed useful now—
A service—yes! and an important one—
A way of touching hearts
For whom the city's streets meant loneliness.
The thought of working there
Filled her all at once with happiness—
With unalloyed delight.

When, on Monday morning, she
    returned to work,
Her heart was floating still—
As if wafted
On joyous waves of inspiration.

    The other women,
Sensing something new around Lisa—
As though some cloud of light enfolded her—
Gathered in little groups,
Eager for gossip.
"What's wrong with Lisa?" they whispered.
A few of them conjectured,
"Perhaps she's in love!"

    But Lisa only smiled.

Then her favorite acquaintance,
Observing how Lisa's thoughts,
Like migrant birds,
Seemed to be soaring to distant lands,
Reflected, "If that girl isn't in love,
She must surely be unwell!"

At lunchtime, she addressed Lisa:
"Child, I must ask you:
Is there some burden on your heart?
You seem so far away from us.
Is something wrong?"

But Lisa only smiled.

That week, however,
As she sat hunched up
Over some new-style,
Shiny button,
She thought often of the golden sun-man.
Would he visit her again?
Ah, *would* he?
Could he forsake her now?
Oh, could he heartlessly withhold the cup
From which she had so lately tasted love?

◆══◆ Four ◆══◆

Sunday came at last,
And with it, good weather.
Lisa, waking late, sat up hurriedly.

High above, the sun's light
Was dimmed by a faint, passing cloud—
As it had been the last Sunday.

Yes! Lisa thought:
There was something in the air!
The atmosphere seemed athrill
With expectancy,
Quiet, vibrant, intense:
The stage seemed set.
Ah! Surely he would return!

Outside the window
A bird sang:
A sweet reassurance, it seemed,
That a few fragile melodies—
Echoes of summer's zephyrs—
Had yet survived the bitter onslaughts
Of approaching winter.

As she sat gazing
In eager anticipation,
The cloud passed,
And the glorious sunlight
Poured once again into the room,
Irradiating its center
With a pool of lambent gold.

Yes! again thought Lisa,
Holding her breath,
Surely from this light streamed
That same mysterious power as before!

Her whole being thrilled with joy
As a cloudlike substance descended,
Drifting gently, like a shower of hope,
Down the shaft of sunlight
To the floor.

Slowly it took shape.

And there at length he stood.
Lisa's heart overflowed:
He had come back!
The golden sun-man had returned
And brought light to her humble dwelling
      once again!

    She knelt before him gratefully,
And the time passed
In a wordless interchange of joy.
Her soul yearned to merge into the bliss
That flowed through him
From some source in Infinity.

After many minutes,
Smiling gently, as if speaking from
Far-off, sun-drenched fields,
He addressed her.

In crystal tones
As of mountain music
He told her of another land—
A land of golden sunshine and laughter,
A realm where love and joy
Formed the very sinews of existence.

    (Strange: Listening to him,
She felt, "I have known this land before!
Was it not mine, too, once—
Eons ago?
Is it not the reflected image
Of some ancient memory—
Faintly visible through the nodding trees
Of more recent, more boldly etched
        impressions—
Glimpses of distant mountain meadows,
Flowering gaily with once-cherished
        joys?")

He had come, he told her,
In answer to her call.

"It was your yearning
For pure happiness,
For crystal love,
That drew me to your sad, misty world.
Your tears could be seen through the night,
Piercing the dark veil of your own forgetfulness.
They rained like dew upon our mountainsides
In glistening showers of light.

"Tell me," he continued gravely,
"How deep is your longing?
Would you leave behind you now—forever—
This prison of lost hopes:
Your lonely city?
Would you exchange your life here
For the shining freedom of my world?"

His world!
Joy in exchange for sorrow!
Gold, for dust!
Her heart cried out with hope.

But the pool of sunlight,
Moving slowly, steadily across the floor,
Bathed her suddenly anew
In the light that encircled him.

Instinctively she drew back,
Ashamed to behold herself—
Mere creature of the city that she was—
Enhaloed in the same light
That surrounded this angelic being.

Glancing up to apologize,
She caught a brief glimpse of his counte-
nance.

He was smiling sadly.

At that moment the sun's blaze
Struck her full in the eyes.
Quickly she lowered her gaze,
Squeezing her eyelids tightly shut.

Then she looked up again—
But he had gone.

And she had not answered him!
Ah, that sad smile!
Was he disappointed with her?
Would he never come again?

Self-accusation alternated with uncertainty:
Both combined to pollute
The crystal springs of ecstasy
That had begun to well up within her.

A fit of weeping seized her.
It lasted the entire day.

⌦ Five ⌫

In the factory that Monday morning
Lisa's work sat heavy on her lap.
Sadly she gazed out the window
At the sunshine as it disported itself
On the grey wall across the street.

Persistently the question echoed in her
 mind:
Had the sun-man left her now—
What a mockery the word seemed!—
Forever?

Slowly, the clouds gathered.
By late afternoon the sky was frowning,
Dark and foreboding.

Observing a kindred darkness
In Lisa's eyes,
Her closest acquaintance thought,
"Well, it may be love,
But more likely this matter is more sinister:
Something must be wrong with that girl!"

At lunchtime, sitting by Lisa's side,
She addressed her.
"This time, girl, tell me—
No, don't look off again
With that migratory smile!—
But tell me *really*:
What is wrong with you?"

And this time,
Though expecting only to be mocked,
Lisa told her tale.

To her surprise,
Her acquaintance took her seriously.
Indeed, she had heard of this man!

"Others there are," she said—
"I've spoken with a few of them—
Who claim to have seen this—
This foreigner in our midst.
Most of them are old now,
But years ago, they claim,
He came to them,
Drifting downward on a shaft of sunlight
Into their dingy homes.

"Like you, they tell of how,
When the light encircling him
Struck them full in the eyes,
He disappeared.

    "I think," she mused,
"They must have been dreaming,
Though it's strange I admit:
That every one of them—
Bent, gnarled old crones,
Stoop-shouldered, misty-eyed—
Dreamed the same dream!"

The acquaintance paused.
"A few of them"—
She looked at Lisa meaningly—
"Dreamed something beyond that.
It seems he wasn't satisfied
With merely coming to them,
But spoke in fluting words,
Inviting them, so it seems"—
She raised an arm in a sarcastic gesture—
"To soar away with him
To some distant, 'never-never' land—
A place he made out to be
Quite unlike this, our own fair—
Or at any rate, quite *real*,
And perfectly normal city!"

"And did they go?" asked Lisa eagerly.
She had said no word
Of the sun-man's invitation.

"No—luckily for them, they stayed."
The older woman sat up.
Smoothing her skirt, she gazed about her
As if severely to affirm
The rightness of their life in the city.
Smugly, then, she continued,
"They were too clever to succumb—
Not *that* far, anyway!
Time passed, and this—'oddity'
Ended his visits.
Well, after all, they had obligations
To their work,
To their lives in the city,
And to the rightful expectations
Of their friends and families.

"A few of them, I suppose—
Such, I'm afraid, is human weakness!—
Wondered as the years passed
Whether, by refusing,
They had not been cowardly.
Perhaps it was their vacillating natures
That first attracted him!
In any case, the facts are clear,
And obvious to everyone of common sense:
It took courage to resist
What was either an idle dream,
Or even worse:
A terrible temptation!

"Ah, well," she concluded,
"What good can there have been
In that strange fantasy?
Uselessly those women try to share it,
Clutching at strangers' sleeves
On crowded streets.
Few stop to listen;
Most shake their clutching hands off
        impatiently.
Yet, if one of them,
Unpressed for time,
Pauses to hear the tale,
Those women only weep."

Lisa said nothing.
Silently, however, she wondered:
Had those tired old women
Done well to refuse?
And if so,
Did she, herself, belong to the city—
And the city to her?

Gradually the doubt grew within her:
Was not her duty *here?*
What, indeed, would her co-workers think
If she abandoned her work at the factory?
Might it not place a strain on them all—
Now especially, in the November winds?
Could a replacement be found?
And would it not be cowardly to flee,
While the city's inhabitants
Prepared themselves bravely
To face the cold of winter?

That week passed
In slow, plodding minutes.
Wednesday, the cutting winds began again,
Driving across the city without mercy.
"It won't be long, now,"
The women said to one another,
Glancing uneasily out the window,
"Before the snows begin."

Lisa sat shivering,
Numb with the cold,
Her little pile of work before her,
Sewing buttons onto men's shirts
With automatic precision.

Often and often, now,
She thought of that coming Sunday,
And prayed longingly
That the sun might shine again—
"Yes, *once* again!"—
That she might, just once more,
Be given the opportunity to decide.

But even then, she asked herself,
"Ah, even if the sun *does* shine—
Will he come?"

He had said she owed his visits
To her own deep yearning
For love and happiness.
Well, but surely her yearning
Was more intense now than it had ever
        been!

But was it?
The doubt returned:
Had her feelings,
All unperceived by her—
Like the fleeting hours
Of nocturnal darkness—
Changed?

He had offered her everything
Her heart had ever craved,
Yet she had drawn back from it—
As if a stranger to it!
Was not this, her very hesitancy,
Proof that she rejected the gift he bore?

She knew, at any rate,
That if his offer was renewed,
She must decide
Where her life truly belonged.

Were perfect love and happiness
Hers *by right?*
Or did she, after all, owe her existence
To the cold, unfeeling city?

Her favorite acquaintance had claimed that
Those women were wise to turn away.
But what, by remaining,
Had they gained?

And what, for that matter,
Had they given?

⊹═⊹ Six ⊹═⊹

Sunday came.
It was late when Lisa woke,
And the sun was high,
Though this time unobscured by any cloud.
Light already filled the room
With a glory well-nigh unendurable.
The girl's heart swelled
As if in a rising, silent hymn
Of faith and hope.

Minutes passed. Then—
A cloudlike shape drifted downward
In the golden shaft.
Slowly the misty figure
Once again took shape.

And there he stood!
To Lisa, he seemed more than ever
Divinely beautiful.

As she knelt before him,
The city ceased for her to exist.
The miracle of his presence
Was all she now knew.
She felt she had been born
Into a wonderful—
Into the only *true*—
Life.

The sun-man, however,
Smiled sadly—
As he had the last time.

"I have asked so many," he said.
"Almost all have refused!
Will you, too,
With burdened heart,
Turn back to your cold,
Unfeeling city?
Is the power of Love too great
For your weak heart, also, to bear?"

Alas! Was that it?
Was it love she had feared,
Not the betrayal of her duty?

Considering anew her heart's dilemma,
She saw now that the city
Cared for her not at all;
Was *incapable* of love for her—
Was incapable of *love*!
How, then, by leaving it,
Could she betray it?

And what was her *highest* duty—
If not to Love itself?

"I love thee!" she whispered.
"Let all that I know and am be drowned
In the ocean of pure love!

"No," she continued, "I am not afraid.
Love only is life.
Without love,
All else is death!"

The sunlight,
Stealing once more—
Slowly, across the floor,
Enveloped her once again
In a blaze of glory.

But this time she welcomed it:
The more so because it encircled also him.
She knew now that she
Belonged to that light,
And that light, to her—
That whatever was outside of it
No longer pertained to her.

Fearlessly she gazed
Into the full brilliance.

And the shaft of light
Moved on slowly—
Across the empty room.

╪══╪ Seven ╪══╪

Back in the factory the next morning
The other women worked,
Sewing buttons onto men's shirts.
Most of them toiled in silence,
Unconscious of the passing time.

After awhile,
One of Lisa's little circle
Looked up, and saw her empty chair.

"Does anyone know where Lisa is?"
She asked. Not waiting for an answer,
She mumbled, "I suppose she's out sick."

A button slipped
From her cold fingers to the floor.
With peering eyes,
She stooped in search of it,
And addressed it sharply with self-concern.
When again she sat up,
Lisa was forgotten.

At lunchtime, another woman commented
On the girl's absence.
Her favorite acquaintance heard—
And wondered.

Yes, wondered—
Though in her heart I think she knew—
Whether the missing girl had, after all,
Dared to leave for another
This most real of all imaginable worlds.